ROAD RALLY

by Leslie McGuire

interior illustrations by
Marie De John

STECK-VAUGHN
C O M P A N Y

CHAPTER

1

It was almost always sunny in Saddle Valley, California, but that was normal. Nearly the whole state of California was usually sunny. Malcolm Frazier was bent over the engine of his car. He was checking hoses, wires, and the oil level. His sister Marsha stood watching him. Malcolm stepped back and admired the shiny red car. It was a 1968 Ford Mustang convertible, a classic hot rod.

"I know I'll win," he thought to himself. "I've got to!"

Malcolm had worked on his car for two years. He had put almost every penny he made working at the local supermarket into buying car parts.

When he first got the Mustang, it barely ran at all. The car was a complete junker. Malcolm had rebuilt the engine, put in new brakes, and changed the gauges.

And he had done all the body work, too. Malcolm had found most of the parts in the junkyard, and now the car ran like magic. The great body work and pinstriped paint job made it look extra cool.

"Did you check the radiator hoses, the brakes, and the tire pressure?" quizzed Marsha.

"Of course I did," Malcolm replied.

Marsha knew a lot about mechanics from watching Malcolm work on his car. She had also watched car races on TV her whole life. The fast-paced excitement kept her eyes glued to the television screen whenever a car race was on.

Marsha had big plans for becoming a race car driver herself someday. Whenever Marsha watched a big race, she imagined herself in the driver's seat. There were all kinds of records just waiting to be broken by a female racer!

Marsha knew that today was very special for Malcolm. It was the day of the big rally car race sponsored by the local auto parts store. The race went from Saddle Valley to Hunterville, Nevada, a town in the Mojave Desert. This race was special. The rules were that the drivers couldn't break the speed limit. The only way to win was to plan the route carefully to avoid traffic and other possible problems.

The prize was a job working in the pits at the Long Beach Grand Prix. Malcolm also wanted to be a race car driver. Working the Grand Prix pits would give him a chance to meet lots of important people in the racing business. Winning this road rally would be a real break.

"So, where's the finish line, Malcolm?" Marsha asked, trying to be helpful.

"Hunterville, Nevada," answered Malcolm. "It's a seven hour trip. You've got to travel through some pretty intense desert landscape. Hot rods like mine can overheat on long desert trips because they're so powerful. But I'm sure my car can make it."

"I know it can," said Marsha.

"Well, I'd better take the car on a test drive before Jim gets here," said Malcolm. Jim was Malcolm's best friend. He was going to be Malcolm's navigator and mechanic. "See you in a few minutes. I'll be back in a flash!"

"Can I come, too?" Marsha asked.

"No way! Are you kidding? The last thing I need is some nerdy fifteen-year-old driving around with me. Forget it!" Malcolm said firmly.

"Come on, Malcolm! I promise I won't get in the way," she pleaded.

Malcolm looked at Marsha standing there. She looked so eager, he felt guilty.

"Okay, but only on one condition!"

said Malcolm. "When we get back, you have to make sandwiches for Jim and me to eat on the trip!"

"It's a deal!" Marsha said with a grin. The brother and sister shook hands. Then Malcolm closed the hood and they hopped into the car. He turned the key, and the powerful engine roared to life.

Marsha remembered when Malcolm had gotten that engine. She had helped put it in. The engine was a used Chevy 454 Big Block. Marsha wasn't a bad mechanic. In fact, Malcolm had actually let her work on the engine. Marsha thought they made a good team when they put their heads together under the hood of a car.

Malcolm carefully pulled the car out of the driveway. As they drove down the street lined with palm trees, they waved to all their neighbors. The route of the test drive took them to the freeway entrance and back.

They drove with the Mustang's top down. Marsha loved the way the wind felt blowing through her hair.

As the two pulled back into the driveway, they saw their mother walk out onto the front porch.

"There's a phone call for you, Malcolm!" she said. "It's Jim."

Malcolm ran inside and picked up the phone. "Hey, pal! How's it going?"

"Not so good," Jim replied in a weak

voice. "I've got a temperature of 103 degrees, and I've already thrown up three times this morning."

Malcolm's heart did a little flip. He knew what was coming next.

"There's no way I can ride with you in the race today," Jim went on. "My doctor says that I need my rest or else I'll get even sicker. I'm sorry, Malcolm, but there's nothing I can do."

Malcolm gritted his teeth in anger. He

13

didn't want to show how mad he was. He tried to think of something nice to say, but it wasn't easy.

"That's all right," Malcolm said in a strained voice. "I hope you feel better, though. I'll give you a call tomorrow to see how you're doing."

Malcolm hung up the phone. He turned to his mom and sister. "Well, I have good news and bad news. The good news is we're not in the middle of a major earthquake."

"What's wrong?" asked Marsha.

"The bad news is, Jim can't come!" Malcolm moaned. "I can't believe this is happening! Now I can't be in the rally. Every driver has to have a mechanic as a partner. I'll never win that job at the Grand Prix! There's no time to find another mechanic!"

CHAPTER
2

"Why don't you ask another one of your friends to be your mechanic?" asked Malcolm's mother. "What about Sammy or Chico?"

"All of them are in the race already," said Malcolm. He threw himself on the couch. "I don't know anyone else who's good with cars!"

"Well, dear, there must be something you can do," his mother said softly.

"What about me?" chimed in Marsha. "Why don't you take me as your mechanic?"

"Are you kidding? What would the other guys think if I brought my little sister along with me?" cried Malcolm.

"Well, if you don't take me, then it looks like you just won't get to race," said Marsha.

Malcolm sat up on the couch and put his head in his hands. Marsha knew he was in deep thought. He always talked quietly to himself when he had big decisions to make. The longer he sat, the more worried he looked.

"Okay, okay. I have no choice. You can

come," Malcolm said gloomily. "But only if you promise not to act like a nerd around my friends."

"All right!" she said with a grin. "Now that I'm your navigator and mechanic, I think we'd better talk about what route we're going to take to Hunterville."

"Why?" asked Malcolm.

"Because I'm the navigator, right?"

"Don't worry about that, little sister," said Malcolm. "I've got it all planned out. We're going to take Route 58 to Highway 15."

"That's a bad idea," said Marsha. "Everybody in the whole race is going to go that way. If we really want to win, we should take Dead Man's Pass straight across. It's much quicker."

"You're crazier than I thought," laughed Malcolm. "Everybody knows that Dead Man's Pass goes right through Death Valley in the Mojave Desert. That's a tough route!"

"Yeah," snapped Marsha, "but it's the only way we can win for sure!"

"If we don't sizzle first!" said Malcolm.

Marsha could see that Malcolm was getting mad. She decided not to say anything else about her plan for now. Besides, they had to get ready.

While Malcolm gave the car one last check and grabbed the maps, Marsha made plenty of sandwiches and filled bottles with water for them to drink. She put in an extra two gallons of water in case of emergencies. Malcolm jumped into the driver's seat and honked the horn.

"Come on!" he yelled to his sister. "Hurry up!"

"Wait a second!" Marsha yelled back. "I need to get something!"

"Don't hold us up, you nerd!" Malcolm said. "We can't be late!"

Marsha ran into her room and pulled

a large gym bag out from her closet. It was a spare parts kit she'd made to give to Malcolm for the race.

Marsha said goodbye to their mother. Then she ran back outside and jumped into the car. She slipped the kit behind her seat and got comfortable.

Marsha had made the kit in case something went wrong with the Mustang during the race. The bag had extra belts, a tire kit, cans of air for flat tires, and a can of oil. She didn't tell Malcolm about it because she knew he would only make fun of her for being a worry wart.

But of course, Malcolm himself worried about being late all the way to

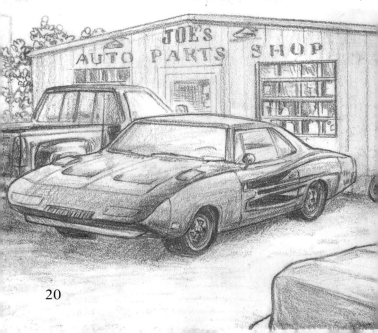

the starting line.

When they arrived in front of Joe's Auto Parts Shop, a few of the racers were already outside talking. Malcolm parked the car and got out.

"You stay here. I don't want my nerdy little sister hanging around when I'm talking to the guys. Sammy, Henry, and Chico are way too cool to hang out with a little kid like you."

Marsha stuck her tongue out at

Malcolm but waited in the car anyway.

She looked over all the cars that were going to be in the race. There were some awesome trucks and some really cool paint jobs. The cars had everything from colorful stripes to flames painted on them.

Fifteen minutes later, Malcolm came back. He looked worried.

"Some of the guys are talking about breaking the speed limit," he said quietly. He got in the car. "If I speed, too, I might get a ticket. Then Mom and Dad would take away my car."

"Speeding is cheating!" said Marsha. "But if we're the only ones not speeding, we won't stand a chance of winning. We'll definitely lose out. What can we do?"

"It looks like our only choice is to try your Death Valley route," said Malcolm.

He reached around to the back seat and grabbed the map. "It's a rough

route. Temperatures can get as high as 125 degrees in that part of the desert. That's really hard for a big engine like this one to take."

Malcolm stared at the map. "But it may be the only way we can win the road rally."

"Then let's do it," said Marsha. "Anything goes, right? If you don't try, you'll never get the pit job at the Grand Prix. It'll be a piece of cake. I mean, what's so bad about the desert, anyway?"

Malcolm knew the desert would be challenging. But he didn't care. He wanted to win! Malcolm started the Mustang and headed for the starting line.

CHAPTER

3

"Racers . . . take your places!" said a voice over the loudspeakers. "The rules of the race are simple: No speeding, no fuzz busters, and no breaking the laws of the road allowed!"

"This is it!" whispered Malcolm. He revved the engine.

As they pulled up to the starting line, Malcolm and Marsha checked out the other cars. Malcolm felt really proud. His car was one of the coolest ones there and he had done all the hard work himself. Marsha felt proud, too. After all, she had helped make the Mustang as cool as it was.

Some of the other cars were pretty awesome, too. Chico was driving a 1969 Dodge Charger Daytona. He'd dropped in an old 8-cylinder Cadillac engine. It was a very fast car.

Sammy was in his 1972 Plymouth Barracuda. Henry was driving a new Chevy 4 X 4 pickup truck. His dad had bought it for him. Henry had never had to work on it. Julio was in his 1967 Camaro with hot flames painted along the side.

The owner of the auto shop waved the green flag. They were off!

There were twenty cars in the race, so it was hard to get ahead right away. A city bus got in the way for a block. To Marsha, it felt like the red lights had never lasted so long in her whole life. It was slow going all the way to the freeway entrance.

The cars began to turn onto the ramp for the southbound freeway. But Malcolm and Marsha stayed on the road they were on and shot past the others. They kept their fingers crossed, hoping no one would notice.

Several blocks later, there were still

no other road rally cars behind them.

"We did it! No one's following us!" laughed Malcolm.

"See! I told you this was the best route to take," said Marsha. "Everyone else has to go south on the freeway for two hours before they get to Wilton Pass. Then they start heading east. This route is mostly just used by freight trucks. Hopefully, no one will think of it. Here comes Dead Man's Pass now. We just cut two hours off the whole trip!"

Malcolm turned on the radio, and they sang along to all the songs. Soon they began to climb the mountains.

"Hey! Look at that sign! We're almost 5000 feet above sea level," Marsha told Malcolm.

"I don't care about sea level!" said Malcolm. "I just wish these slow trucks would get out of my way."

"Don't they understand that we have a race to win here?" asked Marsha.

Neither of them had ever been so high up in the mountains before. The pine trees lining the road were beautiful. But Malcolm and Marsha were glad when they finally started going down the other side. The trucks ahead could go a little faster.

"What are those things?" asked Marsha. She pointed to big mounds of sand by the road.

"Those are sand traps," explained

Malcolm. "If trucks lose their brakes coming down the hill, they just steer into the sand traps. It keeps people from getting hurt."

"Wow!" Marsha said. "It's a good thing you checked the brakes this morning. I'd hate to see what it's like to use those sand traps."

"Just because we're in a car doesn't mean we have nothing to worry about," warned Malcolm.

As they reached the bottom of the mountain, Malcolm pulled into a rest area with a small gas station and a restaurant.

"We'd better fill up before we begin the stretch through the Mojave Desert," Malcolm said. "This is the last place where we can get gas before the race's finish line."

"Good idea," said Marsha. "I'll go inside and get some juice."

Malcolm filled the tank and followed

Marsha into the restaurant. As Marsha was paying for the juice, Malcolm glanced out the screen door. There were two cars from the race at the gas pumps! It was Sammy and Chico! Their navigators jumped into the cars and slammed the doors. The cars took off. Malcolm kicked himself for not seeing them on the road before. He had only been paying attention to what was ahead.

"Hurry up, Marsha!" Malcolm said.

"Okay, okay, give me a break," Marsha snapped. "I'm trying to pay the man for the juice. Hey, how about this fruit-and-nut mix? Do you want some?"

Malcolm exploded. "Sammy and Chico have been following us the whole way! Now they just got ahead of us!" He ran out through the screendoor. Marsha left the right change on the counter and ran after him.

Malcolm stopped dead in his tracks. Marsha gasped when she saw the car.

"The tires! Those cheaters flattened my tires! I don't believe this!" Malcolm moaned. "Now we're out of the race for sure!"

"Well, let's get this car over to the pump and refill those tires, pronto!" Marsha exclaimed.

As the brother and sister pushed the car up to the gas station's air pump, Malcolm noticed something strange.

"Hey! The nozzle for the pump is gone!" he yelled.

"It's got to be around here somewhere," Marsha replied nervously.

She was getting a sick feeling in her stomach.

Malcolm looked all around the pump. He shook his head. "It's not here. Sammy or Chico must have stolen it. This is a nightmare! Now I'll never win!"

"Don't we have a pump in the car?" Marsha asked.

"Yes, we do!" Malcolm snapped. "But it's going to take forever to pump up all four tires."

Marsha began to panic. Then she remembered the kit!

CHAPTER
4

"Don't worry," said Marsha with a grin. "We haven't lost yet."

"What do you mean we haven't lost yet? With four flat tires and only a hand pump, how do you expect us to win now?" Malcolm yelled.

"Lucky for you," Marsha said as she reached behind her seat, "I brought this along."

She pulled out the gym bag.

"Marsha!" Malcolm shouted. "This is no time to be kidding around!" He was getting really mad. "What we need now is an air pump, not your silly old gym bag!"

Marsha pulled several cans of canned air out of the gym bag.

"See? All the air we need is right here in these cans," she said. She handed the cans to Malcolm.

"Oh! Canned air . . ." Malcolm said.

"So? Isn't that good enough?"

"Why didn't you tell me you had this?" he asked as he filled up the right tire in the rear.

Marsha sighed and threw up her hands. "I was trying to tell you," Marsha explained. "But you were too busy yelling to hear what I was saying!"

"Well, maybe I was a bit hard on you. Here, why don't you do one of the tires." Malcolm pointed to the front of the car. "And just wait until I tell the judge of the race about this. Those guys will be thrown out of the car club for good," Malcolm added. He started filling the next tire.

"How can we tell the judge if we aren't even sure which one of them did it?" asked Marsha. "It could be either Sammy or Chico. The only way we would know for sure is if we saw it happen. It wouldn't be right to accuse anyone unless we're sure," she added.

"I guess you're right," said Malcolm. "But it doesn't matter anyway. Both of them are so far ahead of us by now we'll never catch up."

After Malcolm finished filling up the last tire with air, they got back on the road again.

As they drove they could see that they were coming into a huge valley. For two hours there were no trees or shrubs—just flat, sandy earth that went on forever in all directions.

"So this is Death Valley. I hope the car can take the heat out here." Marsha said. "The engine's temperature gauge is already a bit high."

"I know," Malcolm said as he looked at the gauge on his dashboard. A funny noise came from under the hood of the car. He tried to ignore it, hoping it was nothing.

But ten minutes later Malcolm knew something was wrong. "The engine is overheating," he said. "The gauge is all the way to the top!"

They quickly pulled off to the side of the road. Malcolm cut the engine. Then he poured some water from a bottle into a cup for a drink. He jumped out of the car and sat down on the sand. Marsha could tell he was really upset. She got

out of the car and stood next to him. Now that she was out of the moving car, she realized just how truly hot it was.

"Now I know how the car feels. I don't think I've ever been so hot in my whole life!" Marsha said. She looked over at the car.

"I'd better check out the problem and fix it, or we'll never win," mumbled Malcolm.

"Can't we just let the car cool down for awhile? This is a serious situation," said Marsha.

"It's not just overheated," said Malcolm. "The car was making a funny sound when we pulled over. I'll get to it in a second," said Malcolm, without looking up. "But I'm way too hot and thirsty to stand over the engine right now! I need a water break."

"Well, I don't know about you, but I don't feel like being stranded out in this desert," said Marsha. "We haven't seen another car since we left the restaurant. That was an hour and a half ago. Who knows how long it will be before another car finds us if we can't fix the Mustang. I'm going to take a look," she added. Marsha walked back to the car.

She popped the hood open and looked at the engine for a moment.

"Come on, Malcolm! Even I can fix this," she yelled. "It's a broken fan belt!

It's a piece of cake to fix!"

"Wrong," mumbled Malcolm. "I don't have a new fan belt. Jim was supposed to bring replacement parts. I forgot to get them when I found out he wasn't coming."

"No problem," said Marsha. She walked to the side of the car to get her emergency kit. "I've got one right here!"

But as Marsha reached into the back of the car, she heard a strange rattling sound near her feet.

Marsha looked down to see a deadly rattlesnake coiled near the right back tire. Its mouth was open. The tip of its tail whipped back and forth in a blur. The snake's poison-filled fangs were headed right for her ankle!

"Malcolm!"

CHAPTER
5

Seeing the snake, Malcolm threw his cup of water as hard as he could at it. The snake slithered off into a pile of rocks as Marsha stumbled backwards.

"Are you okay?" Malcolm asked.

"Whew!" said Marsha, sitting down. "That's the scariest thing that ever happened to me. That snake was going to bite me!"

"You're lucky," said Malcolm softly. "Why don't you get in the car while I put on this belt. Then we'll get out of here."

"Hurry, before the snake comes back. And if anything rattles . . . run!" Marsha said. She felt very shaky.

Malcolm had the belt replaced in no time. He hopped back into the car and they were off.

They had been driving for an hour when Marsha noticed a car stopped by the side of the road up ahead.

"Look!" she said. "Somebody's stopped up there."

"You're right," said Malcolm. "And I'd know that car anywhere. That's Chico!"

"Why do you think he stopped?" asked Marsha.

"Maybe it's another trick," said Malcolm.

As they got closer, they could see Chico opening the hood of his car. A big white cloud rushed out.

"Wow!" said Marsha. "Did you see all that smoke?"

"That's not smoke," said Malcolm. "That's steam. Steam blows out of the radiator when the engine gets too hot."

"Will his car be okay?" asked Marsha.

"It'll be fine in an hour," explained Malcolm. "First the engine needs to cool down. Then it will need water added to it. That will make up for the water it lost when it blew out the steam."

"Should we give him our extra bottle of water?" asked Marsha.

"I don't know," said Malcolm. "What if he was the one that flattened our tires? Does he deserve our help?"

"Well," Marsha began, "we can't be sure he's the one who flattened our

tires. And even if he did, so what! If we don't help him, that would make us just as bad as the person who flattened our tires."

Malcolm frowned as he pulled up behind Chico's car. Then he said, "I guess you're right. You might as well give him the extra water. It's dangerous out here."

Marsha darted over to Chico and his navigator with the bottle of water.

"Will you two be all right?" she asked them in a worried voice.

"We'll be fine now that the car won't run dry," Chico answered with a smile. "But you guys should hurry if you want to win this race."

As Marsha ran back to the car and hopped in, Chico waved and yelled, "Good luck!" The Mustang's spinning tires screeched on the asphalt. They were on their way again.

"I wish we knew how far ahead Sammy was," said Malcolm an hour later.

"Me too," said Marsha. "We'd know how close we are to winning."

"Hunterville can't be too far from here," Malcolm said. "We're almost out of the desert."

"I'll bet it was Sammy who flattened the tires," said Marsha.

"Why?" asked Malcolm.

"Chico would have looked more

ashamed if he had done it," said Marsha. "Besides, he even wished us good luck on the race."

"It's possible," said Malcolm. "But, hey, look at that." He pointed up ahead to where a car sat parked in front of a policeman's motorcycle.

"It's Sammy!" Marsha cried. She started laughing. "He's getting a speeding ticket!"

"All right! We're sure to win now!" said Malcolm. He pounded on the steering wheel with delight. "The only way Sammy can get ahead of us now is if he breaks the speed limit again!"

"I don't think he'll ever try that again," giggled Marsha.

"Especially not when that policeman is behind him," added Malcolm. He waved cheerfully as they drove past.

By now they could see Hunterville in the distance. "Wow!" said Marsha. "It's weird to see a big city just plopped right down in the middle of a big, empty desert!"

"They must spend all their money on air conditioning," said Malcolm.

"I'll bet! It's like an oven out there," said Marsha.

The Mustang pulled off the highway. "Look at the map and find the main strip in town," said Malcolm at a stop sign. "That's where the finish line is."

Marsha studied the map for a minute. "We're in luck," she said. "This road goes straight to it!"

"Excellent!" said Malcolm. He was so excited that he had a hard time staying at the speed limit. It took five minutes to get to the main strip.

"There's the finish line!" said Malcolm. "See the yellow ribbon stretched across the street?"

"Yup. I see it," Marsha said sadly as the Mustang closed in on the yellow ribbon. "The problem is, I see Henry's 4 X 4 there, too. How'd he beat us?!?"

CHAPTER
6

Henry stood at the finish line with a smile on his face. He had his hand resting on the trophy at the judge's table. It looked like Henry would be getting the Grand Prix job that Malcolm wanted. Malcolm felt as if his dreams had just been washed down the drain.

"I don't believe this," Malcolm said. "After all we went through, we lost anyway. It just isn't fair!"

"At least we tried our hardest," said Marsha. She tried to comfort Malcolm.

"But where is everybody else?" said Malcolm suddenly. He had a curious look on his face.

"Maybe there was a traffic jam," said Marsha. She reached towards the radio. "Let's turn on the traffic report and see."

"A huge jam up still has Wilton Pass at a stand still," said the radio announcer's voice.

"Wow! Malcolm! Listen to this!" Marsha cried.

"There has been a tractor-trailer collision. Traffic hasn't moved for the past two hours," continued the voice.

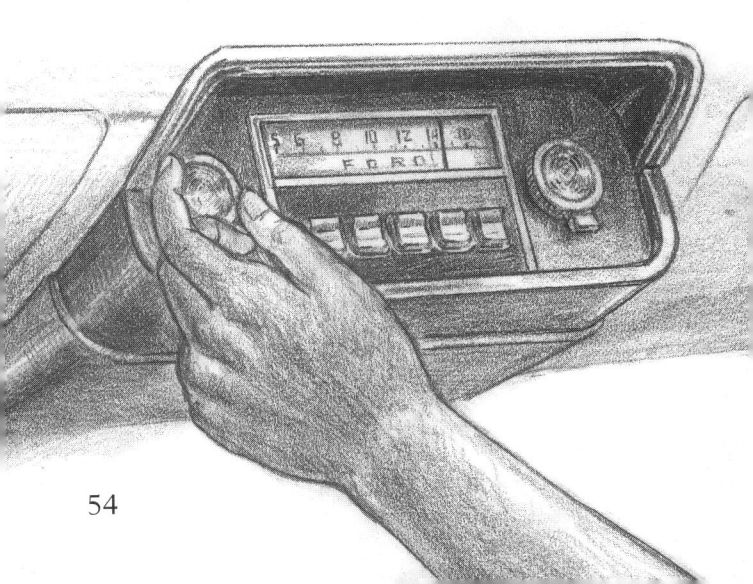

"Anyone planning to leave California by that route had better find another way."

"So, that explains where everybody else is," said Malcolm. "They're stuck on Wilton Pass."

He parked the Mustang near the finish line. "I'm going over to go talk to Henry's navigator, Frank," Malcolm. said. He and Marsha got out of the car.

"I'm going to go to the bathroom," said Marsha. She went into a restaurant across the street from the finish line.

As she walked towards the back of the restaurant, Marsha saw Henry. He was dialing a number on the pay phone outside the bathroom. She slipped into the bathroom before he had a chance to see her. From inside the bathroom, she could hear him talking.

"Hi, Dad. This is Henry," he said into the phone. "Yeah! We won!"

There was a moment of silence, then Henry went on. "But we wouldn't have

been able to do it without that fuzz buster you bought me. It worked really well! There was a big traffic jam on Wilton Pass. So I just put the truck in four-wheel drive and drove on the shoulder of the road. I would have been ticketed if the fuzz buster hadn't showed me where the police cars were hiding."

Marsha was shocked. So that's how he had gotten so far ahead of the rest of the racers! That explained why nobody else from the race was here except Henry. She waited until he left. Then she ran to Malcolm.

"Come here, Malcolm! We have to talk!" Marsha hissed. She grabbed her brother's arm and pulled him away from Frank.

"You numbskull! What's wrong with you?" snapped Malcolm. "Can't you see I'm talking to someone here?"

Marsha didn't listen. She just kept pulling him away from Frank.

When they were out of earshot, she whispered, "Just listen to this! Henry cheated! And I know how we can prove it!" Marsha told him what she had heard in the restaurant.

"Okay. Let's go find the judge and tell him," said Malcolm.

Marsha and Malcolm headed for the grandstands. There were people milling all around. Reporters had come from the local newspaper. Friends and families of the race-car drivers were waiting for all the cars to cross the finish line.

"Do you see the judge?" Marsha asked. "I'm having a hard time seeing over this crowd of heads."

"I think he's over in the stands to the left," Malcolm replied. "Let's try to head in that direction."

Marsha and Malcolm worked their way through the crowd. Finally they spotted the judge. He was a large man, wearing the bright red official judge's jacket. He was still sitting in the stands.

Marsha hurried up the steps of the grandstand. "Excuse me, sir," she said to the judge.

The judge turned his head and smiled at Marsha. "Yes, young lady. How may I help you?" the judge replied.

"Isn't it against the rules of the race to

use a fuzz buster?" asked Malcolm.

"And isn't it also against the race rules to break the law of the road?" added Marsha.

"Why, yes," the man said. "You're both right. Why do you ask?"

"We believe that Henry, the winner of the race, broke both of those rules," said Malcolm. "My sister overheard him talking on the phone about using a fuzz buster. He used it to speed on the shoulder of the freeway. That way he could pass the traffic jam in Wilton Pass. Can you look in his truck to see if there is a fuzz buster in there?"

They followed the man over to Henry's truck. Henry was just getting ready to leave.

"Excuse me, Henry," the judge said. "We have a tip that you used a fuzz buster in the race. May I take a look inside your truck?"

"Sure," said Henry. He threw up his

hands. "I have nothing to hide."

The judge climbed in and looked around. Then he went to the other side of the truck and looked some more.

"I don't see anything," he said to Malcolm and Marsha.

"Maybe it's hidden someplace!" Marsha urged.

"Why don't you just shut your mouth and stop lying!" sneered Henry. "You're just jealous because you weren't good enough to win. I'm no cheater, and you know it!"

"Yes, you are!" Malcolm yelled.

"Then where is the evidence?" Henry snapped back.

"Right here!" boomed the judge. They all looked over.

The judge stood holding up the fuzz buster. "I just found this tucked way back under the seat of your truck, Henry. It looks like you just lost the race and your membership in the car club," he said.

Henry hung his head in shame. "You're right," he mumbled. "I cheated."

The judge frowned at Henry. Then he broke into a smile. "Congratulations, Malcolm Frazier! You are the winner of

Check out these other exciting
▼ STECK-VAUGHN Adventures!

Get ready for a bumpy ride! Travel on
SNAKE RIVER

Where there's smoke. . . there's fire
Read all about it in
SMOKE

Is there any truth to the old pirate's poem?
Find out in
FORGOTTEN TREASURE

Are they tough enough to rough it?
Check out the boys who
DON'T LOOK BACK

Is the big prize worth a big risk?
Get the answer in
VIDEO QUEST

Danger lies where eagles soar. Find out why in
SOARING SUMMER

Knight makes right? See how in
KNIGHT MOVES

The chase is on — but who's hunting who?
Find out, read
DANGEROUS GAME

A family can survive anything, right?
Learn more in
SNOW TREK

7 8 9 10 06 05 04 03 02

Produced by Mega-Books of New York, Inc.
Design and Art Direction by Michaelis/Carpelis Design Assoc.

Cover illustration: Wayne Alfano